EARLY AMERICAN HISTORY

The 13 Colonies

By Bert Wilberforce

Published in 2024 by Cavendish Square Publishing, LLC
2544 Clinton Street Buffalo, NY 14224

Website: cavendishsq.com

Library of Congress Cataloging-in-Publication Data

Names: Wilberforce, Bert, author.
Title: The 13 colonies / Bert Wilberforce.
Other titles: Thirteen colonies
Description: Buffalo, New York : Cavendish Square Publishing, [2024] |
Series: Inside guide : early American history | Includes bibliographical references and index.
Identifiers: LCCN 2022053417 (print) | LCCN 2022053418 (ebook) | ISBN 9781502667816 (library binding) | ISBN 9781502667809 (paperback) | ISBN 9781502667823 (ebook)
Subjects: LCSH: United States–History–Colonial period, ca. 1600-1775–Juvenile literature.
Classification: LCC E188 .W613 2024 (print) | LCC E188 (ebook) | DDC 973.2–dc23/eng/20221108
LC record available at https://lccn.loc.gov/2022053417
LC ebook record available at https://lccn.loc.gov/2022053418

Editor: Therese Shea
Designer: Deanna Paternostro

The photographs in this book are used by permission and through the courtesy of: Cover, p. 10 Everett Collection/Shutterstock.com; p. 4 kojihirano/Shutterstock.com; p. 6 (top) iofoto/Shutterstock.com; p. 6 (bottom) The-Lost-Colony 0/Wikimedia Commons; p. 7 Zack Frank/Shutterstock.com; p. 8 Indenture - Servitude 1823/Wikimedia Commons; p. 9 GezichtOpNieuwAmsterdam/Wikimedia Commons; p. 12 The Mayflower Compact 1620 cph.3g07155/Wikimedia Commons; p. 13 Cultivation of tobacco at Jamestown 1615/Wikimedia Commons; p. 14 1670 virginia tobacco slaves/Wikimedia Commons; p. 16 Plimoth Plantation 2002/Wikimedia Commons; p. 18 Harvard Old College/Wikimedia Commons; p. 19 Tryon Palace/Wikimedia Commons; p. 20 SavannahColony/Wikimedia Commons; p. 21 (main) House of Burgesses in the Capitol Williamsburg James City County Virginia by Frances Benjamin Johnston/Wikimedia Commons; p. 21 (inset) Patrick Henry Rothermel/Wikimedia Commons; p. 22 Indigenous American Nations, 16th century - 2022 edition/Wikimedia Commons; p. 24 Marcio Jose Bastos Silva/Shutterstock.com; p. 25 Brookfield1/Wikimedia Commons; p. 26 NorthAmerica1762-83/Wikimedia Commons; p. 27 Map of territorial growth 1775/Wikimedia Commons; p. 29 (left) Interview of Samoset with the Pilgrims/Wikimedia Commons; p. 29 (right) Courtesy of the Library of Congress.

CPSIA compliance information: Batch #CSCSQ24: For further information contact Cavendish Square Publishing LLC at 1-877-980-4450.

Printed in the United States of America

CONTENTS

Chapter One: Beginnings	5
Chapter Two: Reasons for Colonization	11
Chapter Three: Life in the Colonies	17
Chapter Four: A Time of War	23
A Timeline of the British Colonies	28
Think About It!	29
Glossary	30
Find Out More	31
Index	32

The Native Americans had highly developed societies when the Europeans arrived to explore. The Cliff Palace in today's Colorado was occupied by the Ancestral Pueblo peoples from around 1150 to 1300 CE.

BEGINNINGS

By the time Europeans came to the Americas, Native Americans had lived there for thousands of years. However, these lands—this New World—seemed an amazing discovery to the Europeans. They began exploring the Americas at the end of the 1400s.

Many early explorers were interested in finding riches. Others wanted to trade with Native Americans. Still others, for many reasons, were searching for a new home. The most successful settlers of North America were the British. Their 13 colonies became the foundation of the United States of America.

The Roanoke Mystery

The British attempted to build a permanent settlement in North America in 1587, following two unsuccessful tries. About 150 people settled on Roanoke Island in present-day North Carolina. After a time, the new settlement needed supplies. They waited, but no ships came. Finally, the governor of the island—John White—sailed to

The first permanent European settlement in North America was St. Augustine, Florida, which was settled in 1565 by the Spanish.

Britain for supplies. Conflicts between Spain and Britain kept White from returning immediately. He was delayed several years.

When White finally arrived back on Roanoke Island in 1590, there was no sign of the colonists. All that remained were messages—"CRO" and "CROATOAN"—carved into trees near the settlement.

Fast Fact

Spain claimed Florida at first. Between 1763 and 1783, Florida belonged to Great Britain. Spain then took it over, but **ceded** it to the United States in 1821.

No one knows for sure what happened to the colonists of Roanoke Island, though it might have something to do with nearby Croatoan Native Americans or their island, also called Croatoan.

Jamestown

In 1607, about 105 settlers from Britain arrived in the Virginia colony and founded Jamestown. Jamestown was the first permanent British settlement in North America. In the first years of the community, most of the colonists died as a result of hunger, disease, and battles with Native Americans.

However, Jamestown did not disappear like the settlement on Roanoke Island. It was able to succeed with the help of the Powhatans and provisions arriving by boat. The colonists of Jamestown were able to pay for supplies by growing tobacco and selling it to people in Britain.

Fast Fact

Pocahontas was the daughter of Powhatan, the chief of an **Indigenous** community near Jamestown. She married settler John Rolfe in 1614.

Jamestown later burned—twice. Today, the U.S. National Park Service maintains the site.

INDENTURED SERVANTS

The first European **indentured servants** arrived in the British North American colonies soon after Jamestown was settled. Europeans who could not afford the cost of the trip could enter into a contract with a colonist. The colonist paid the cost of the person's voyage to America. In return, the traveler agreed to be an indentured servant, usually for four to seven years. Some preferred having indentured servants to hiring other colonists. Indentured servants were required by law to work, whereas other colonists could leave a job. Some indentured servants were treated poorly. Others received money or land after their contract was done.

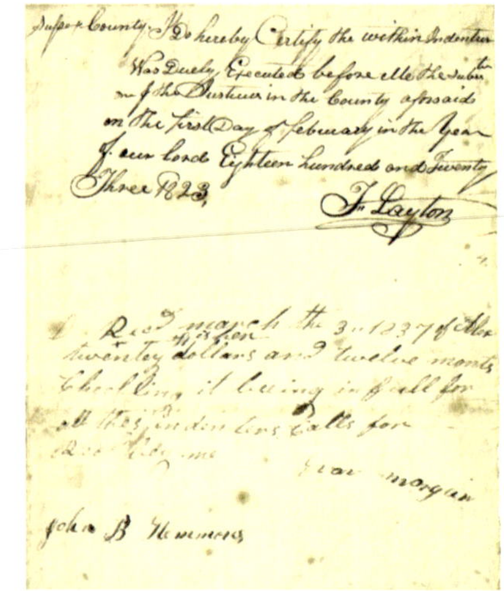

Sussex County We do hereby Certify the within Indenture Was Duely Executed before Me the subscriber one of the Justices in the County aforesaid on the first Day of February in the Year of our Lord Eighteen hundred and Twenty Three 1823

J. Layton

This document binds a six-year-old child named Evan Morgan to 14 years of indentured servitude.

Other Europeans

Great Britain was only one of the numerous European countries to settle North America. Besides Florida, Spanish settlements were mainly to the west of the British colonies. The French settled in large numbers in present-day Canada and along the Mississippi River, and they were a big presence in the current state of Louisiana. The Dutch settled along the Hudson River. The biggest Dutch settlements were New Amsterdam, which later became New York City, and Fort Orange, which became Albany.

The British took possession of the Dutch colonies in 1664, after the governor of New Amsterdam surrendered without a fight. The French almost totally disappeared as a result of the French and Indian War (1754–1763). The Spanish presence in North America continued until the 1800s.

This is a 1664 illustration of New Amsterdam, now Lower Manhattan in New York City.

Christopher Columbus, shown here with his crew, came upon the so-called New World while looking for a western trade route to Asia.

REASONS FOR COLONIZATION

People had many reasons for settling in North America. For some, religion was a motive. They wanted a place to freely practice their faith without fear of **persecution**. Protestants from France, known as Huguenots, settled in the British colonies to escape religious persecution. Many Germans settled in the British colonies to flee the Thirty Years' War (1618–1648), a conflict between Catholics and Protestants. A now-famous group of British settlers were also inspired to seek religious freedom.

The Pilgrims of Plymouth

In the early 1600s, a group of Puritans called Separatists became unhappy with the Protestant church in Britain. Unlike most Puritans who wanted to "purify" the Church of England, the Separatists wanted to separate from it. Today, we know this group as the Pilgrims.

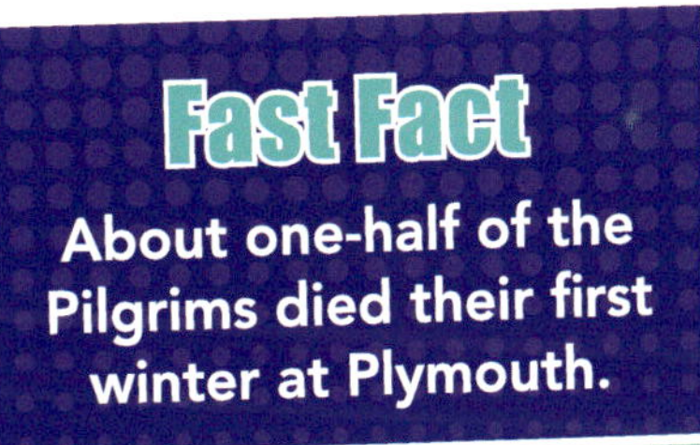

At first, they moved to Holland, but they soon thought a better life awaited over the Atlantic, in the British colonies. The ship *Mayflower* left Plymouth, England, in September 1620. The travelers meant to reach today's New

About 35 of the 102 travelers on the *Mayflower* were Separatists. All would later be called Pilgrims.

York but landed around Cape Cod in Massachusetts in November. They founded the first permanent settlement in New England, called Plymouth.

In Search of Wealth

Many people came to the colonies in search of wealth of any kind. Colonists acquired land, grew crops, and raised animals.

The colonies became an important part of the British Empire. They provided **raw materials** to Britain and in return bought British goods. The New England colonies in the North—later called Massachusetts, New Hampshire, Rhode Island, and Connecticut—sold fish and whale oil to Europe. New England's trees were used as lumber for shipbuilding. Colonists from the middle colonies—today's New York, New Jersey, Pennsylvania, and Delaware—sold animal furs and crops such as corn and wheat. In the southern colonies—modern Virginia,

Before the Jamestown settlement found that tobacco grew well there, the settlement nearly collapsed because early colonists spent so much time looking for gold.

Fast Fact

Great Britain passed a law stating that any criminal sentenced to death could be sentenced to work in the colonies. Other unwilling colonists were actually kidnapped.

Maryland, North Carolina, South Carolina, and Georgia—the valuable crops were tobacco, rice, and **indigo**. The success of certain crops meant farmers looked for more labor.

Slavery Takes Hold

In 1619, the first enslaved Africans came to the colonies, specifically Virginia. However, until the early 1700s, the number of willing and

This image from 1670 shows enslaved people working on a Virginia farm.

THE TRIANGULAR TRADE ROUTE

The triangular trade route describes the roughly triangular shape of trade between three regions. It centered on the buying and selling of enslaved Africans. Africans were taken from Africa across the Atlantic Ocean to the Americas. Crops and raw materials were then taken from the Americas to Europe for trade. Finally, European goods, including guns, were shipped to Africa to purchase more enslaved Africans. As many as 12 million enslaved Africans were transported forcibly to the Americas this way. Many died from the terrible conditions onboard the ships. In 1808, the young United States banned the importing of enslaved people—but not slavery itself.

Fast Fact

At first, some enslaved people were treated as indentured servants, but they were later stripped of all rights. Their children were born into slavery too.

unwilling workers coming from Europe was enough to meet labor needs. In fact, white servants were less expensive than enslaved people. Eventually, the colonies wanted more workers than Europe could provide. The number of enslaved people greatly increased. Many were sent to the South, where they worked on large farms.

Enslaved people did not have the rights that indentured servants had. They could be bought and sold. They had to work for as long and as hard as their enslaver wanted.

Plimoth Patuxet in Massachusetts has created homes in the style of Plymouth in the 1600s.

LIFE IN THE COLONIES

Colonists began new lives in their communities. They worked and had families, and the settlements grew. They gave their communities in the British colonies much the same structure as the villages, towns, and cities they came from.

Colonial Education

At first, colonial children were taught at home. Then, the colony of Massachusetts ordered the establishment of the first public schools. These schools were supported financially by their communities. Students were taught to read and write. They also learned Latin, Greek, and other subjects. Schools were attended mostly by boys. If girls went to school, it was only for a few years.

As religion was an important part of colonial life, especially in the New England colonies, the first colleges were set up to train **clergy**. These were called divinity schools. Wealthy students interested in pursuing other professions, such as law or medicine, usually returned to Great Britain to study.

The first college in the British American colonies was Harvard, started in the city of Boston, Massachusetts, in 1636.

Colonial Governments

At the beginning of the colonial period, the British government allowed the colonies a great amount of self-governance. One reason for this was that several early colonies were established by businesses. British companies obtained permission to settle certain parts of America without interference from other businesses. For example, the Virginia Company of London (or London Company) was given a **charter** in 1606 to found

The governor of each British colony acted as the representative of the British king. Sometimes the governor was at odds with the colonial legislatures. Pictured here is the Governor's Palace (or Tryon Palace) in North Carolina.

Fast Fact

The British government left its American colonies to deal with their own affairs until the mid-1700s. This policy is called salutary (useful) neglect.

settlements on the eastern coast of North America. The colony of Virginia resulted from this. Other colonies, such as Pennsylvania, were given by the British king to pay off debts.

After a colony was established, a governor was appointed with the power to select officials and to suggest and revoke, or put an end to, laws.

Each colony had a legislature, or lawmaking assembly. Nearly all the assemblies were composed of two bodies. The upper house was appointed by the colonial governor to serve as his advisers. The lower house was a representative body of the colony elected by voters. Usually, this lower house made the local laws.

THE 13TH COLONY

James Oglethorpe headed a group of British officials who sought to find a home in the British colonies for imprisoned debtors of "good moral character." At the time, British people were put in prison if they could not pay back money they owed. In 1732, Oglethorpe received a charter to colonize land between the Savannah and Altamaha Rivers. Oglethorpe founded the colony of Georgia in 1733, naming it for King George II, and governed it until 1743. Georgia also welcomed Protestants from Austria and Germany. Oglethorpe helped organize forces to defend the colony against the Spanish to the south who also claimed the land.

At first, the Georgia colony did not allow slavery. However, restrictions were later lifted.

Fast Fact

Only white men who owned property could elect representatives to colonial legislatures.

Distance made colonial governments necessary. During the colonial period, the only way to travel across the Atlantic Ocean was by boat. The trip between Great Britain and the British colonies took 8 to 12 weeks. A colonist might have waited 6 months to receive a letter. It was difficult to make any but the biggest decisions in Britain. The first British colonial representative assembly was was formed in 1619 in Jamestown.

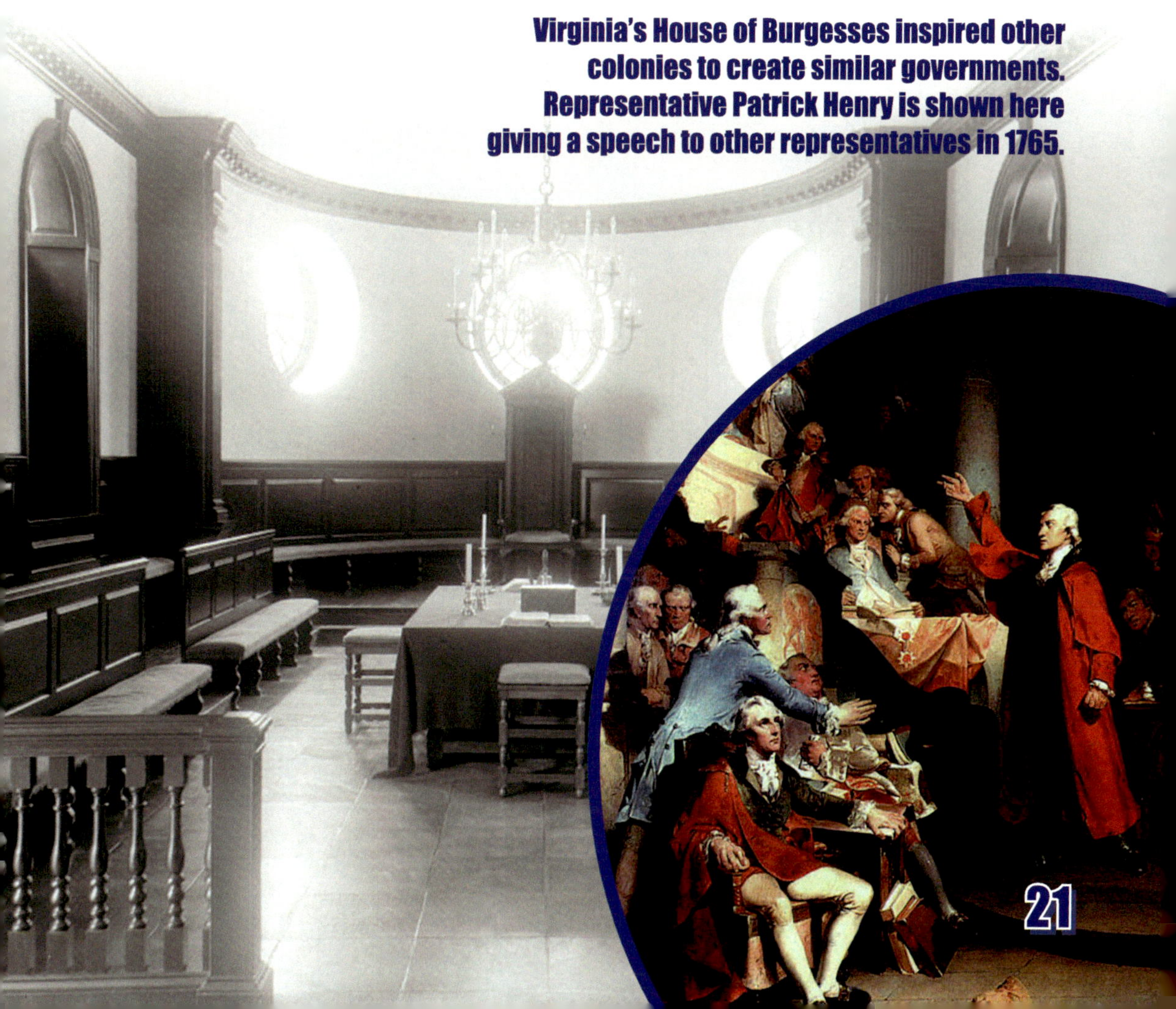

Virginia's House of Burgesses inspired other colonies to create similar governments. Representative Patrick Henry is shown here giving a speech to other representatives in 1765.

This map suggests how diverse Indigenous peoples were in the 1500s, before the colonization of North America.

A TIME OF WAR

In many parts of the British colonies, life was not peaceful. Some of this unrest was rooted in the souring relationships between the colonists and the Native Americans who had long called North America home. Even those European colonists and Indigenous peoples who had fostered friendly relations at first found themselves at odds while competing for resources.

Indigenous Issues

Native Americans often regarded the colonists warily. In some regions, they viewed them as a threat and attacked. In others, they were accepting and helped colonists adjust to life on the new continent. They showed them how to raise corn and other crops, and where to fish and hunt. In return, the colonists provided goods Native Americans could not make, such as guns, gunpowder, and metal tools.

> **Fast Fact**
>
> Colonists brought diseases that killed millions of Indigenous people. An estimated 90 percent died of illnesses such as flu, measles, and smallpox.

However, good relations became strained as the number of colonists

Ousamequin, known to colonists as Massasoit, was a sachem, or chief, of the Wampanoag **confederacy** of New England. He welcomed the Pilgrims in 1621.

grew and they moved deeper into Native American lands. There were several wars between the colonists and Native Americans throughout the colonial period. Native Americans were eventually forced out of much of the British colonial lands.

The War Before the War

The largest war between Great Britain and France in North America—known as the French and Indian War—began in 1754. Both sides had support from Native American **allies**. The British were eventually able to block communication between France and its North American colonies. This, along with the capture of Montreal in Canada, led to the Treaty of

KING PHILIP'S WAR

After the death of Ousamequin (Massasoit), his son Metacom became the leader of the Wampanoag. The growing population of British colonists and their movement onto more and more Native American land angered Metacom. The British also wanted the Wampanoag to surrender their guns. In 1675, the colonists hanged several Native Americans, sparking the beginning of a war fought throughout present-day Connecticut, Rhode Island, Massachusetts, and Maine. As the British called Metacom "King Philip," it is often called King Philip's War. Both sides raided towns and villages. The war ended in August 1676 with Metacom's capture and death.

Thousands of Native Americans were killed in King Philip's War. Many were enslaved as well.

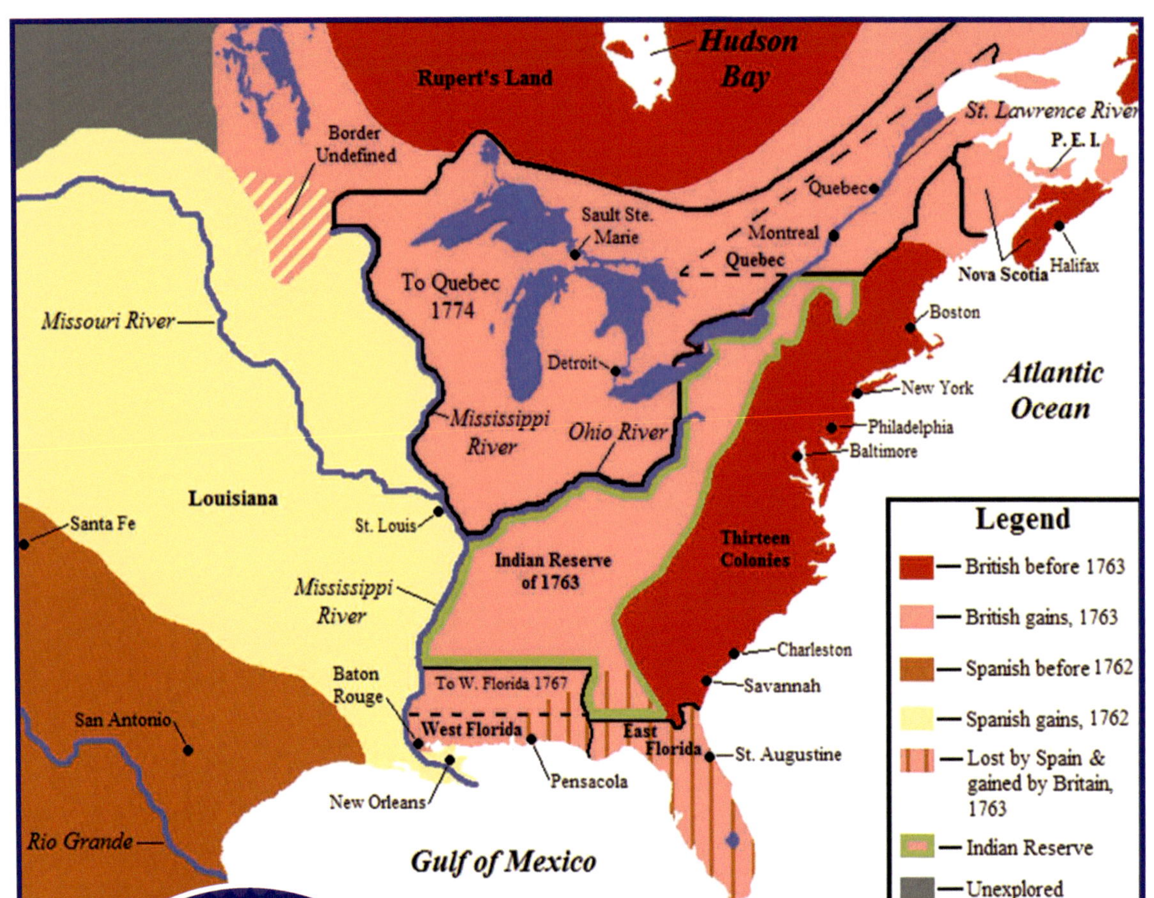

This map shows the land Britain and Spain gained after the French and Indian War.

> **Fast Fact**
>
> In 1800, Spain secretly ceded Louisiana back to France. But in 1803, French emperor Napoleon sold it to the United States.

Paris in 1763. France surrendered all land in North America to Britain and Spain.

With the defeat of the French and their Native American allies following the French and Indian War, the French were no longer a danger to the colonies. The colonists did not need the might of the British army to defend their borders from the

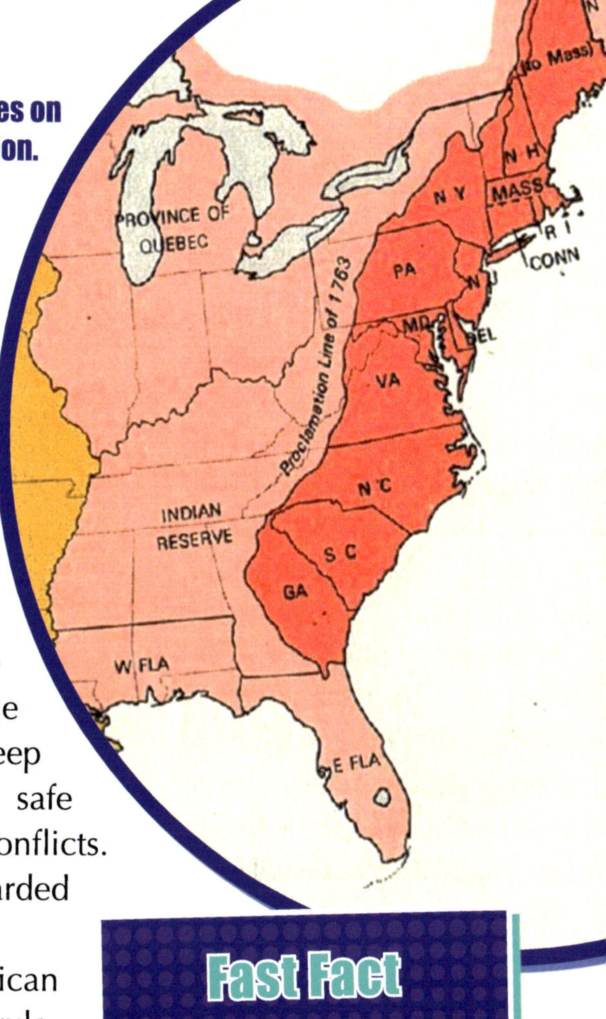

In this map, you can see the 13 colonies on the eve of the American Revolution.

French anymore. Britain wanted the colonists to pay for the war and for their own defense, and so taxed them to raise money, angering many colonists.

In 1763, a British **proclamation** was issued stating colonists could no longer settle lands west of the Appalachian Mountains. The land was to be reserved for Native Americans. The proclamation was also meant to keep colonists and Native Americans safe from each other and prevent conflicts. Colonists quickly disregarded the proclamation.

By the 1770s, many American colonists wanted complete self-rule. The American Revolution would begin in 1775, at the Battles of Lexington and Concord in Massachusetts. The former British colonies of North America would then become the United States.

Fast Fact

The American colonies had the support of France and Spain in the American Revolution.

A TIMELINE OF THE BRITISH COLONIES

1587 Settlers arrive on Roanoke Island in Virginia.

1607 Colonists arrive at the Jamestown site.

1619 The first colonial assembly forms in Jamestown. The first enslaved Africans land in Virginia.

1620 Pilgrims establish Plymouth in Massachusetts.

1623 David Thomson settles near today's Portsmouth, New Hampshire.

1634 Settlers led by Lord Baltimore settle in today's Maryland.

1636 Harvard University is established. Roger Williams founds Rhode Island.

1663 King Charles II gives British nobles control of the Carolina province.

1664 The Netherlands surrenders New Netherland (including parts of New York, New Jersey, Pennsylvania, Maryland, Connecticut, and Delaware) to Great Britain.

1676 The death of the sachem Metacom ends King Philip's War.

1681 William Penn is given a charter for a colony that becomes Pennsylvania.

1733 James Oglethorpe establishes the 13th colony, Georgia.

1763 The French and Indian War ends with the Treaty of Paris.

1776 The British colonies declare independence.

THINK ABOUT IT!

1. Why was the printing press at Harvard an important contribution to the British colonies?
2. Why do you think some early settlements were successful while others were not?
3. Why do you think Native American groups sided with France or Great Britain during the French and Indian War?
4. Do you think Great Britain's decision in the mid-1700s to exert more direct control over the colonies had a part in the American Revolution? Why or why not?

GLOSSARY

ally: One of two or more people or groups who work together.

cede: To give, often by treaty.

charter: An official agreement giving permission to do something.

clergy: A leader in religious services.

confederacy: Two or more groups in an agreement of support.

indentured servant: One who signs a contract agreeing to work for a set period of time in exchange for money or other benefits.

Indigenous: Having to do with the first people in an area.

indigo: A plant with spikes of red or purple flowers, or the blue dye that comes from it.

persecution: Making a group of people suffer cruel or unfair treatment.

proclamation: A public announcement.

province: A large division, or part, of a country.

raw material: Something that is used to make or create something.

FIND OUT MORE

Books

Honders, Christine. *The Real Story Behind the 13 Colonies*. New York, NY: PowerKids Press, 2020.

Turner, Amanda. *The Slave Trade in Colonial America*. Broomall, PA: Mason Crest, 2020.

Uhl, Xina M. *Colonialism*. New York, NY: Rosen Central, 2020.

Websites

British America: Thirteen Colonies
www.dkfindout.com/us/history/american-revolution/british-america-thirteen-colonies/
Use an interactive map to find out more about each colony.

Colonial America
www.ducksters.com/history/colonial_america/thirteen_colonies.php
Read interesting facts, such as how the colonies got their names, and take a quiz.

Thirteen British Colonies
education.nationalgeographic.org/resource/resource-library-thirteen-british--colonies
Check out these important links to learn more about the 13 colonies.

Publisher's note to educators and parents: Our editors have carefully reviewed these websites to ensure that they are suitable for students. Many websites change frequently, however, and we cannot guarantee that a site's future contents will continue to meet our high standards of quality and educational value. Be advised that students should be closely supervised whenever they access the internet.

INDEX

A
American Revolution, 27

C
charters, 18, 20
Connecticut, 12, 25

D
Delaware, 12
Dutch, 9

E
enslaved people, 13, 14, 15

F
France, 9, 11, 24, 26, 27
French and Indian War, 9, 24, 27

G
Georgia, 13, 20

H
House of Burgesses, 21

I
indentured servants, 8, 15

J
Jamestown, 7, 8, 13, 19, 21

K
King Philip's War, 25

L
legislatures, 19, 21

M
Maryland, 12
Massachusetts, 12, 16, 17, 25, 27
Metacom, 25

N
Native Americans (Indigenous peoples), 4, 5, 6, 7, 22, 23, 24, 25, 26, 27
New Hampshire, 12
New Jersey, 12
New York, 9, 11, 12
North Carolina, 5, 13, 19

O
Oglethorpe, James, 20
Ousamequin (Massasoit), 24, 25

P
Pennsylvania, 12, 19
Pilgrims, 11, 12, 24
Plymouth, 11, 12, 16
Pocahontas, 7

R
Rhode Island, 12, 25
Roanoke Island, 5, 6, 7
Rolfe, John, 7

S
slavery, 15, 20, 25
South Carolina, 13
Spain, 6, 9, 20, 26, 27

V
Virginia, 5, 7, 12, 13, 14, 19, 21